This igloo book belongs to:

....

Contents

igloobooks

Published in 2017
by Igloo Books Ltd, Cottage Farm, Sywell, NN6 0BJ
www.igloobooks.com

Illustrated by Maxine Lee
Written by Melanie Joyce

Designed by Justine Ablett
Edited by Jenny Cox

STA002 1017
4 6 8 10 9 7 5 3
ISBN 978-1-78670-005-6

Printed and manufactured in China

5 Minute Tales

Farm Stories

igloobooks

Cock-a-Doodle-Oink!

Rooster woke the animals early one day on Merry Dale Farm.

Cock-a-Doodle-Doo!

"We've got to get ready for the Big Farm Show tomorrow,"

he said.

So, everyone got busy **washing** and **brushing** and **polishing**.
All except Duckling, Piglet, and Calf, who ran around playing chase.

Oink-oink went Piglet, **slipping** and **skidding**. He **splattered** mud on Dog and **tumbled** into Calf, who **crashed** into Duckling who **knocked** over the water bucket.

Cock-a-Doodle-Doo!

"Behave yourselves. Otherwise you won't go to the show,"

said Rooster.

Duckling, Piglet, and Calf **didn't** listen to Rooster.
All day long, they chased each other **around** and **around**.
By the afternoon, everyone was fed up with them.

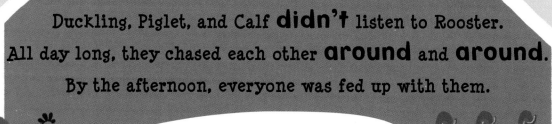

"**Stop messing around!**"

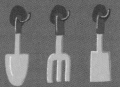

cried Rooster, just as Piglet **knocked** over a
milk urn, which got **stuck** on Cow's foot.

Cow **bellowed** and **frightened** Duck...

6

... who **flapped** and **panicked** the mice...
... who **squeaked** and **spooked** Horse...

... who **neighed** and **startled** Pig...
... who **squealed** and **scared** Cat.

There was complete chaos on Merry Dale Farm.

COCK-A-DOODLE-DOO!

went Rooster, as **loudly** as he could.

"Off to bed with you three!"

said Rooster, puffing up his feathers in the most alarming way.

Duckling, Piglet, and Calf **slunk** off to bed, realizing that they should have done as they were told.

"We won't be allowed to go to the show now,"

said Calf.

Calf thought for a while.

"I've got an idea. Why don't we get up early tomorrow morning and be extra quiet? Everyone will see we can behave ourselves, then we will be allowed to go to the Big Farm Show!"

he said.

Early next morning, Duckling, Piglet, and Calf crept across the farmyard, but all they could hear was **snoring** and **snorting**.

"They're still asleep," whispered Duckling.

Then they saw Rooster strutting around with his beak wide open, but with **no sound** coming out!

"He's lost his voice!" said Piglet.

"It must have been all that shouting yesterday," said Calf.

"We'll have to wake everyone up. All together now, one... two... three..." said Duckling.

QUACK-A-OINK-OINK-MOO!

Suddenly, everyone woke up.
"You've saved the day!" said
Horse, as she quickly got ready.
"Come on, there's just enough
time to get to the show."

"Well done, Duckling,
Piglet, and Calf.
You can come to the
show, after all,"

whispered Rooster
in a croaky voice.

12

Everyone had a **super** time at the Big Farm Show, especially Duckling, Piglet, and Calf. Just for once, they were allowed to make as much **noise** as they liked... and they **loved** it!

QUACK-A-OINK-OINK-MOO!

Little Chick's Big Adventure

One day, Little Chick and Mother Hen went to the meadow where Horse was grazing near the woods.

"what are the woods like?"

asked Little Chick.

"The woods are scary,"

said Horse.

"Never go there by yourself,"

said Mother Hen.

But this just made Little Chick all the more **curious.**

14

Mother Hen and Little Chick **pecked** and **scratched** until Mother Hen settled down to roost. Just beyond the fence, Little Chick could see the woods.

As his mother fell asleep, he took one tiny step towards them. Nothing bad happened, so he took another.

In the woods, there were little streams and pretty flowers where bunnies **hopped** and squirrels **scampered**.

Little Chick played chase with the bunnies...

... and hide-and-seek with the squirrels.

The woods aren't **scary** at all, thought Little Chick.

All afternoon, Little Chick
played with the woodland
animals until it was time
for them to go home.

"Goodbye,"

he called.

"Goodbye, Little Chick,"

they said.

Suddenly Little Chick felt sleepy. He snuggled
down for a nap in the warm afternoon sun.

HOO-HOO! came a noise. Little Chick opened his eyes. The sun had gone and the sunny paths were crossed with **shadows.** Little Chick didn't know which way to go. He began to feel **cold.** He began to **shiver.**

HOO-HOO! Owl swooped down.

"Are you lost?" she asked.

"Yes," whispered Little Chick as he looked into Owl's big eyes.

"I can show you the way home,"

she said, swiveling her head.

"Let me show you,"

said another voice.

Fox stepped out from the shadows. He **grinned** at Little Chick, showing his **sharp**, shiny teeth.

As Fox and Owl came closer,
Little Chick felt very afraid.

"Mommy was right.
The woods are scary
and I should have
listened to her,"

he thought.

Just then, there was a
stomping and
squawking sound...

... It was Horse and Mother Hen! "Thank you, Owl and Fox," said Horse, politely. "We will take Little Chick home."

Mother Hen hugged Little Chick close.
"Don't ever go off without me again," she said.
"I won't," said Little Chick, as he thanked Mother Hen and Horse. Little Chick had learned a big lesson.

The Goat Detectives

chomp, chomp, **Chomp** went Daisy the goat,
eating Farmer Bill's prize-winning roses,
one morning.

"Mmmm, these are absolutely yummy,"

she said.

"Try the red ones, Daisy. They're positively delicious!"

said Myrtle.

Just then, Farmer Bill came out of the barn. His face went a sort of purply red, just like a **beet**, and he seemed to be in a very **bad** mood.

"Mrs. Bill has put me on a diet. Yet here you two are, eating everything in sight. You can go on a diet, too,"

he said, grumpily.

Myrtle and Daisy didn't like their diet one little bit. It was nothing but lettuce leaves and carrots all week long.

By Sunday morning, their tummies were **rumbling** and **gurgling** so much, they hardly noticed the terrible **commotion** coming from the henhouse.

CLUCK! SQUAWK!
went the hens.

"Someone has taken our eggs!"

"Mrs. Bill will be furious!"

The hens **flapped** their wings and ran around like headless chickens.

"Hmm. This is egg-xtra-ordinary. I think we should investigate. It'll take our mind off food,"

said Daisy.

That night, Myrtle and Daisy
crept into the farmyard.

"Look, footprints!"

said Myrtle.

They followed the trail and it led to the henhouse,
where they saw a shadowy figure putting eggs into a sack.

26

There was a soft **clumping** and a **creaking** as the shadowy figure crept away.

"Let's follow the thief,"

whispered Myrtle,
creeping along behind.

The footprints led to
the farmhouse door.
Very carefully, Daisy and
Myrtle opened it and guess
who they found?

Farmer Bill!

"I was so hungry. I just wanted a few eggs. Anything but lettuce and carrots,"

he said.

Everyone felt sorry for Farmer Bill. Mrs. Bill promised he could stop dieting if he did more exercise. So Farmer Bill promised the goats nice food if they stopped **munching** his roses.

Daisy and Myrtle agreed and Farmer Bill gave them **delicious** things to eat. The hens got their eggs back, and Farmer Bill went jogging every day.

At last, **everyone** was happy on Red Rose Farm.

You Can't Do It Donkey

When the mail arrived at Little Farm one morning,
it caused quite a stir.

"There's going to
be a talent competition
at the town hall
on Saturday,"

cried Goose.

The animals **whooped**, **cheered**, and **chattered**
excitedly, then rushed off to rehearse their acts.

Donkey heard all the **hullabaloo** and came to see what it was about. In the sty, the pigs were practicing their act.

OINK! SQUEAK!

they went, **diving** and **splatting** into **gloopy** mud.

"Can I join in?"

asked Donkey.

"Oh no, donkeys can't dive,"

said the pigs.

So, Donkey visited the cows.
MOO, MOO! they went, **swishing** their tails and **twirling** like great big ballerinas.

"Can I join in?"

asked Donkey.

"Oh no, donkeys don't dance,"

replied the cows.

So, Donkey went to see the sheep.

BAA, BAA! went the sheep, as they practiced their daring high-wire act.

"Oh, that looks exciting. Can I have a turn?"

said Donkey.

The sheep got such a **shock**, they **slipped** and **fell** into the pond.

"Oh no, donkeys don't do daring things,"

they said.

33

On the farmhouse steps,
Goose was tap dancing.

HONK! HONK!

Donkey didn't even bother
asking if he could join in.
"Everyone thinks I'm just a
stupid donkey," he thought.
"Well, I'll show them."
He trotted off to the barn and
closed the doors firmly shut.

Soon, there were some very peculiar noises coming from the barn. **Thumps** and **twangs** and **sploshing** sounds. It was all very strange.

BANG! OUCH! BUMP!

WHOOSH! OOMPH! HEE-HAW!

"Donkey is so silly!"

"It's a good thing he's not in the talent show tomorrow,"

said the other farm animals, laughing.

The next day at the talent show, all the animals performed their acts. At the very end, a late entry was announced. "It's the... er, rather unusual, Donkey," said the announcer. Donkey trotted onto the stage...

... and pretended to be the animals on Little Farm.

The pigs... **HEE-OINK!**

The cows... **HAW-MOO!**

The sheep... **HEE-BAA!**

And lastly, Goose... **HEE-HONK!**

Donkey didn't win the competition, but he
did show everyone exactly what he could do.

The Great Escape

Farmer Claire was doing her best to cheer up the animals on Willow Tree Farm, but it wasn't working. Rodney the horse was tired of his stable, Millicent the cow kept complaining about the cowshed, and Lulu the sheep was sick of her pen.

"Nice food, warm beds. It's not such a bad life, is it?" asked Farmer Claire. No one answered, so she sauntered off.

"What we need is change. What we need is adventure!"

said Rodney.

Everyone agreed, but they weren't sure what sort of adventure.

39

Then, very early the next day, something **amazing** happened. A traveling circus drove right by Willow Tree Farm.

"That's it! We'll run off and join the circus," cried Rodney, snorting.

That's exactly what they did. They packed some snacks and snuck off when Farmer Claire wasn't looking.

Lulu was going to be a trapeze artist, Rodney was going to be a show horse, and Millicent was going to be an acrobat.

They were quite sure that it just meant **swinging** on a few ropes, a bit of **cantering** around, and **bouncing** on a trampoline or two. Life in the circus was going to be easy! But the animals of Willow Tree Farm were in for a nasty surprise...

Ding-a-ling! went the alarm
clock at dawn the next day.

"Time to practice!"

cried the ringmaster.

Rodney cantered around and around until he felt **dizzy**.
Millicent kept **falling** off the trampoline and Lulu was
afraid of heights. All day long they practiced and each
night they performed in the show. By the end of the week,
the animals of Willow Tree Farm were exhausted.

"You all need to work harder. Make sure tonight's show is a really good one!"

said the ringmaster.

"I miss Farmer Claire,"

said Rodney.

"Me too,"

said Millicent.

"Me three,"

added Lulu.

They all decided that they were thoroughly **miserable** with life in the circus.

44

That night, the crowd **roared** and **cheered**. Then, the lights dimmed. Rodney did his usual cantering around and Millicent tried to stay on the trampoline. Then, the ringmaster announced the grande finale. Lulu had just begun to swing on the trapeze when she spotted Farmer Claire sitting in the front row of the audience.

45

Lulu took one hoof off the trapeze, went flying through the air and suddenly lost her grip.

Boing! Millicent bounced high into the rafters.

46

Bang! Millicent landed on Rodney's back and gave him such a fright, he **bolted** around the ring after the ringmaster. Farmer Claire and the crowd fell over laughing. The ringmaster, however, wasn't quite so happy.

"You aren't quite cut out for the circus. I think it's time you went home,"

he said.

The animals agreed and before they knew it, they were back on Willow Tree Farm. Rodney trotted and cantered around, Millicent happily chewed grass, and Lulu lazed in the sun.

"Welcome home,"

said Farmer Claire, with a grin.

She suspected there would be no more adventures for quite some time.